PUBLISHING LTD

Licensed exclusively to Top That Publishing Ltd
Tide Mill Way, Woodbridge, Suffolk, IP12 1AP, UK
www.topthatpublishing.com
Text copyright © Julia Hubery 2014
Illustrations copyright © Tide Mill Media
All rights reserved
0 2 4 6 8 9 7 5 3 1
Printed and bound in China

Written by Julia Hubery
Illustrated by Gill Guile

ISBN 978-1-78244-537-1

A catalogue record for this book is available from the British Library

Little Bear's Big Adventure

By Julia Hubery

'For Mum, who loved my surprises' Julia Hubery

'What shall we do today,
Little Bear?' asked Mother Bear.

Little Bear peeked out of their
shady cave at the hot sun.
'Can we stay here, where it's lovely
and cool?' he asked.

'If we do that, we will have
nothing to eat,' said Mother Bear.
'But I have an idea. Shall we go
somewhere as cool as a cave,
where there's lots of food
we can catch and pick?'

Little Bear jumped up and down, 'Where is it? What will we catch? What will we pick?' he asked.

'It's a surprise,' laughed Mother Bear, 'but here's a clue. What is your favourite pudding?'

'Strawberries?!!'
Little Bear shouted.

'YUM, let's go!'

Little Bear made up a song as he skipped along.

'Mummy and me on a mystery tour,
I hope it's cool and not too far.
We're going to make a wonderful tea,
with scrumptious, yumptious **strawberries!**'

But as the day got hotter, Little Bear became **tired** and **grumpy.**

'**This isn't very cool!**' complained Little Bear, as Mother Bear stopped on a high, rocky ledge in the sun.

'Hush, come and look – here's your surprise,' said Mother Bear.

Little Bear climbed up beside her, and looked down.
Shining out of the forest, like a silver moon
in a deep green sky, was a beautiful, cool pool.

'Hurray!'

yelled Little Bear.

They followed a stream which
bubbled from the rocks,
splashing into rainbows
as it tumbled **down ...**

down ...

down ...

… and into the pool.

The water was icy-fresh and delicious, and Little Bear **loved** it.

'First we'll have a little rest,' said Mother Bear,
'then I'll teach you to fish, and we'll pick
our strawberries, and soon ...'

'… We'll have a perfect picnic!' shouted Little Bear.
Little Bear snuggled up with Mother Bear in the
mossy shade, but he was too excited to nap.
'I will surprise Mummy,' he thought,

'I'll make the perfect picnic myself!'

'Strawberries first,' he said, for he knew the
little nooks where wild strawberries love to grow.
When he had enough for two hungry bears,
he arranged them carefully on a leaf.
'Now, I must catch fish,'
said Little Bear.

He looked at the tumbling stream, and he looked at the quiet pool. 'If I were a fish,' he thought, 'I would hide in the cool pool.' Little Bear peered into the still, deep water. *At first he saw nothing, then … did something move in the shadows?*

Flik-flak, a flash of silver darted by!

Little Bear stretched out to grab the fish,
and as he did, he saw a reflection in the water!

Something **huge** ...

and **dark** ...

and **HUNGRY** ...

was reaching out
to **GRAB** him!

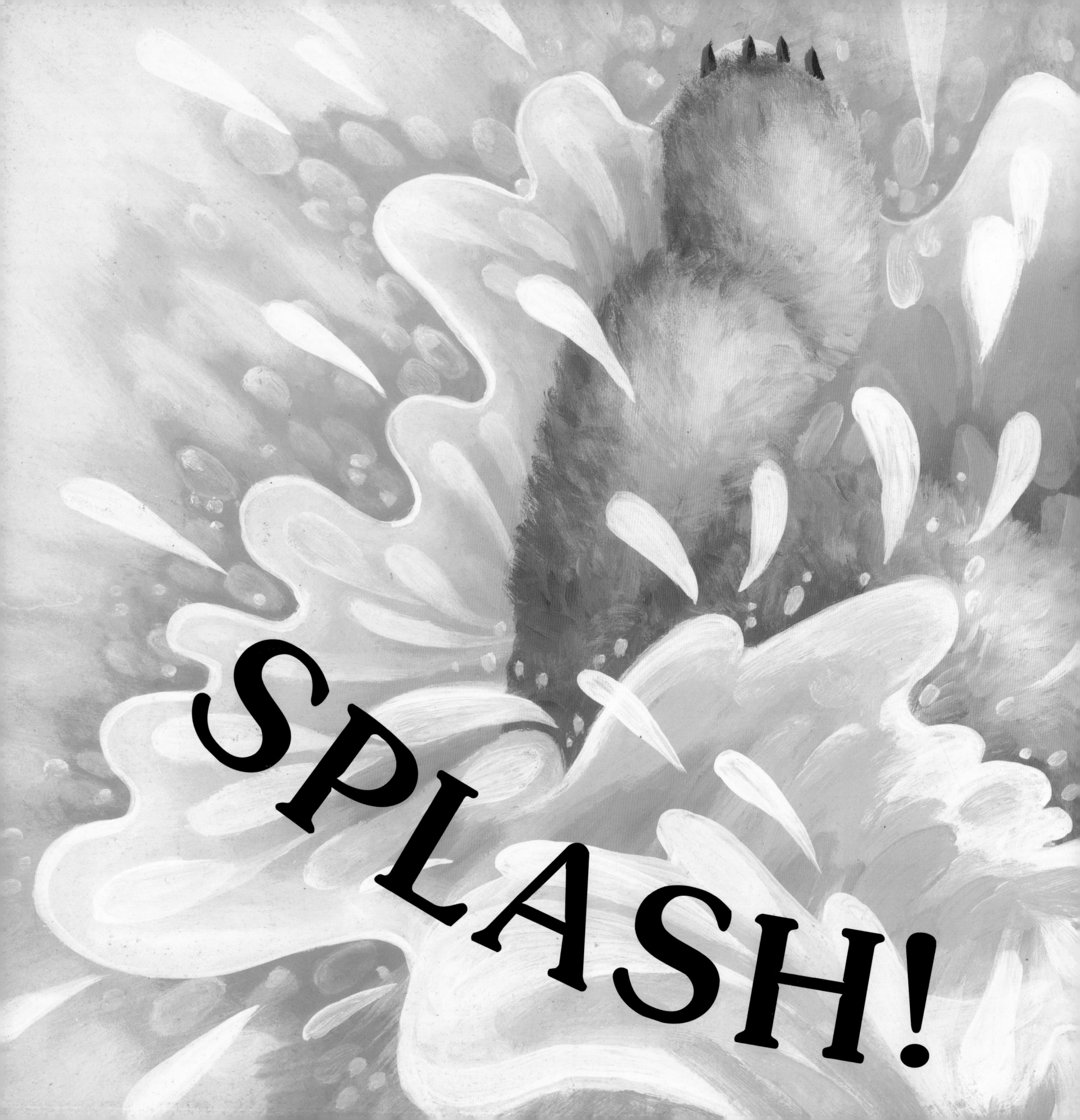
SPLASH!

Little Bear lost his balance,
and toppled into the pool.

Down ...

down ...

down ...

he sank.

The huge dark
creature jumped in after him!

Little Bear struggled
to escape, but strong
hairy arms grabbed at him,
caught him, held him tight
and pulled him from the pool.

Little Bear wriggled
free and saw …

… Mother Bear!

'Mummy!' he cried. 'Where is the B-big H-hairy Sc-scary **Thing** that grabbed me?!!'

'I am the Big Hairy Scary **Thing!**' she laughed.

'I only wanted to make you a wake-up surprise,' said Little Bear.

'That was a kind idea,' smiled Mother Bear, 'but surprises are tricky. You must be careful, or nasty surprises get mixed up with the nice ones!'

Mother Bear gave him a big, soggy hug ...

... and found there was one
more surprise for them both!